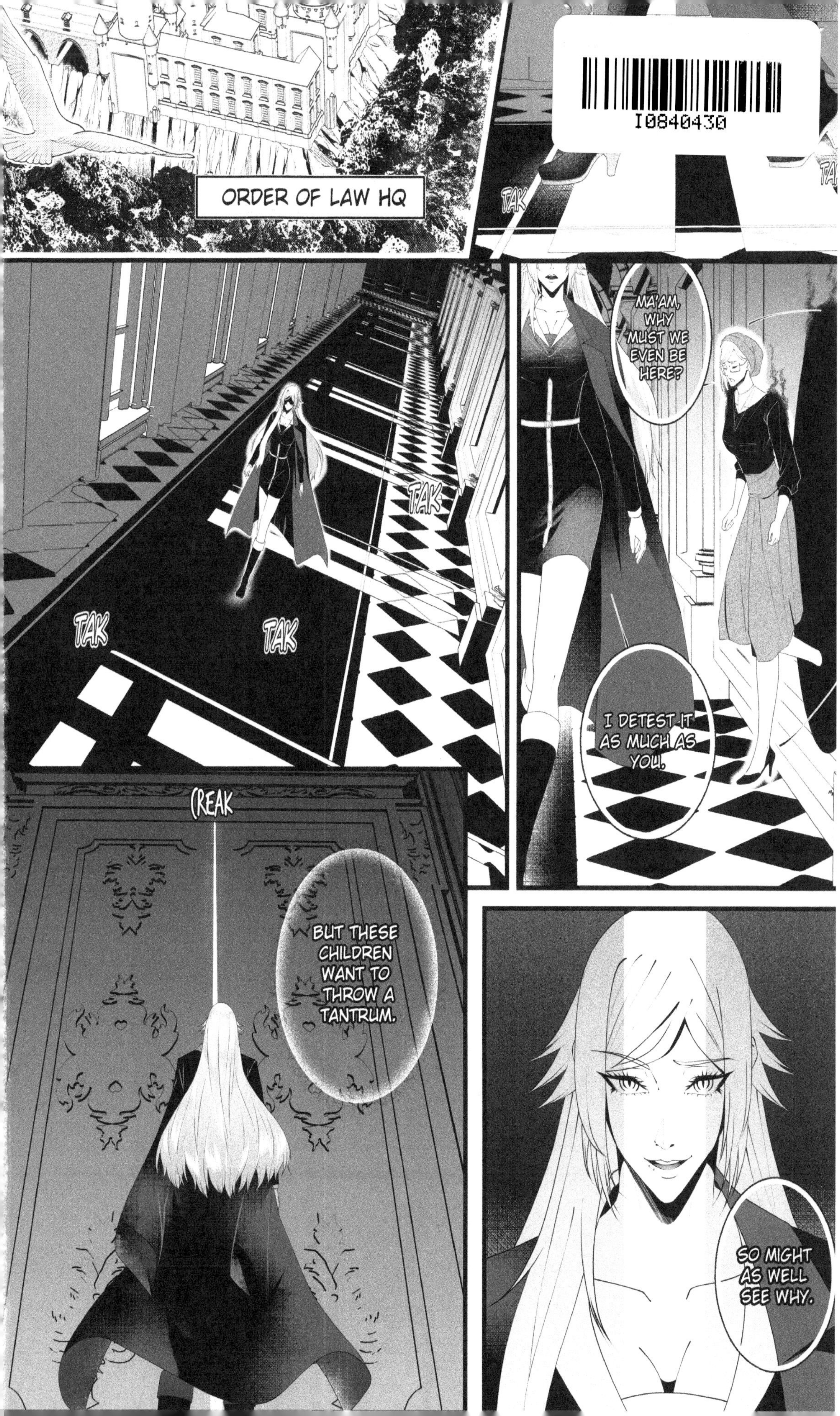

ORDER OF LAW HQ

CREAK

GOOD EVENING LADIES AND GENTLEMEN.

VICE WARDEN OF NIX PRISON:
NORVAL VADEL

WARDEN OF THE NIX PRISON:
JOSHUA TRUTH

I GUESS WE SHOULD GET THIS STARTED EH CHIEF.

ORDER OF LAW CAPTAIN:
SLATE GOPE

ORDER OF LAW CAPTAIN:
JEAN IERA

VERY WELL. TAKE YOUR SEAT.

ORDER OF LAW CHIEF COMMANDER:
JUDAS

HONESTLY I FEEL THIS MATTER COULD OF BEEN RESOLVE OVER THE PHONE.

WELL YOU SEE... WE FEEL THAT YOU WITHHELD SOME.. INFORMATION.

THE 8TH CROWN WAS ABSENT FOR 20 YEARS. YET YOU KNEW EXACTLY WHERE IT WAS AND DIDN'T MENTION IT UNTIL NOW!

SO THIS IS ABOUT THE CROWN RAGO, OR NIGHTSTAR AS YOU LIKE TO CALL HIM.

I THINK THE REAL QUESTION WE HAVE IS, CAN A CRIMINAL BE A CROWN?

HE SHOULD BE STRIP OF HIS CROWN TITLE IMMEDIATELY!
AND WHO SHOULD I GIVE THE CROWN TO THEN... YOU?
SO WE JUST LET THIS "STAREN" ROAM FREE? IF HE BECOMES A "GREAT KING", HE'LL BE PARDONED FOR HIS CRIMES!
I GUESS I HAVE TO SPELL IT OUT TO YOU ALL.
THUDD!!

SNAP

"WHOMEVER RECEIVES THE CROWN IS ELIGIBLE TO BECOME STAR KING, AS LONG AS THEY ARE THE RIGHT AGE."

THESE WERE THE RULES THAT BOTH THE ORDER OF LAW AND THE ORDER OF KINGS AGREED TO.

SO NIGHTSTAR RAGO HAS THE RIGHT TO BE A CROWN WHEN HE TURNED 19.

NOW YOU'RE MORE THAN WELCOME IN TRYING TO TAKE THE CROWN FROM HIM.
BUT IF REACHES SUMMI THEN HE ON NEUT GROUN

I KNOW THIS PUTS A HOLE IN YOUR PLANS JUDAS, BUT YOU WILL FOLLOW MY RULES.
SLAM
WE CAN'T LET THIS GET OUT OF HAND. IF YOU SEE NIGHTSTAR, CAPTURE HIM AT ALL COST.
TO THINK THE KID HAS THE WHOLE WORLD AFTER HIM AT THAT AGE.

WHAT DID SHE MEAN BY "PUTTING A HOLE IN HIS PLAN"?
CHIEF JUDAS HAS BEEN EYEING THE CROWN POSITION FOR A LONG TIME NOW.
YOU DON'T SAY.
OH BEFORE I FORGET.
WHAT'S THIS?
MY TRANSFER LETTER. I'M TRANSFERRING TO ANOTHER PRISON.
WAIT YOU CAN'T LEAVE! WHO WILL PUT THE PRISONERS IN LINE!
YOU KNOW, YOU SHOULD CONSIDER JOINING THE HUNTER UNIT.
O REA

A'AM
HAT
E WE
DING
D DO?
WE'VE DONE OUR PART, NOW WE JUST WATCH THE FIREWORKS.
SHE SCARED ME SOMETIMES ...
VITRO CASTLE GARDEN
SO I TAKE IT DIDN'T GO WELL.
STEP
STEP

CHIEF JUDAS.
NO IT DID NOT.

EVEN I CAN NOT OVER TURN ZAYLA'S LAW.
DON'T WORRY. WE HAVE TIME UNTIL THE SUMMIT.

IT APPEARS THAT NIGHTSTAR MIGHT BE MORE TROUBLE THAN WE THOUGHT.
HE'S ALREADY TAKEN OUT ROMA'S MAYOR.

WHAT?!

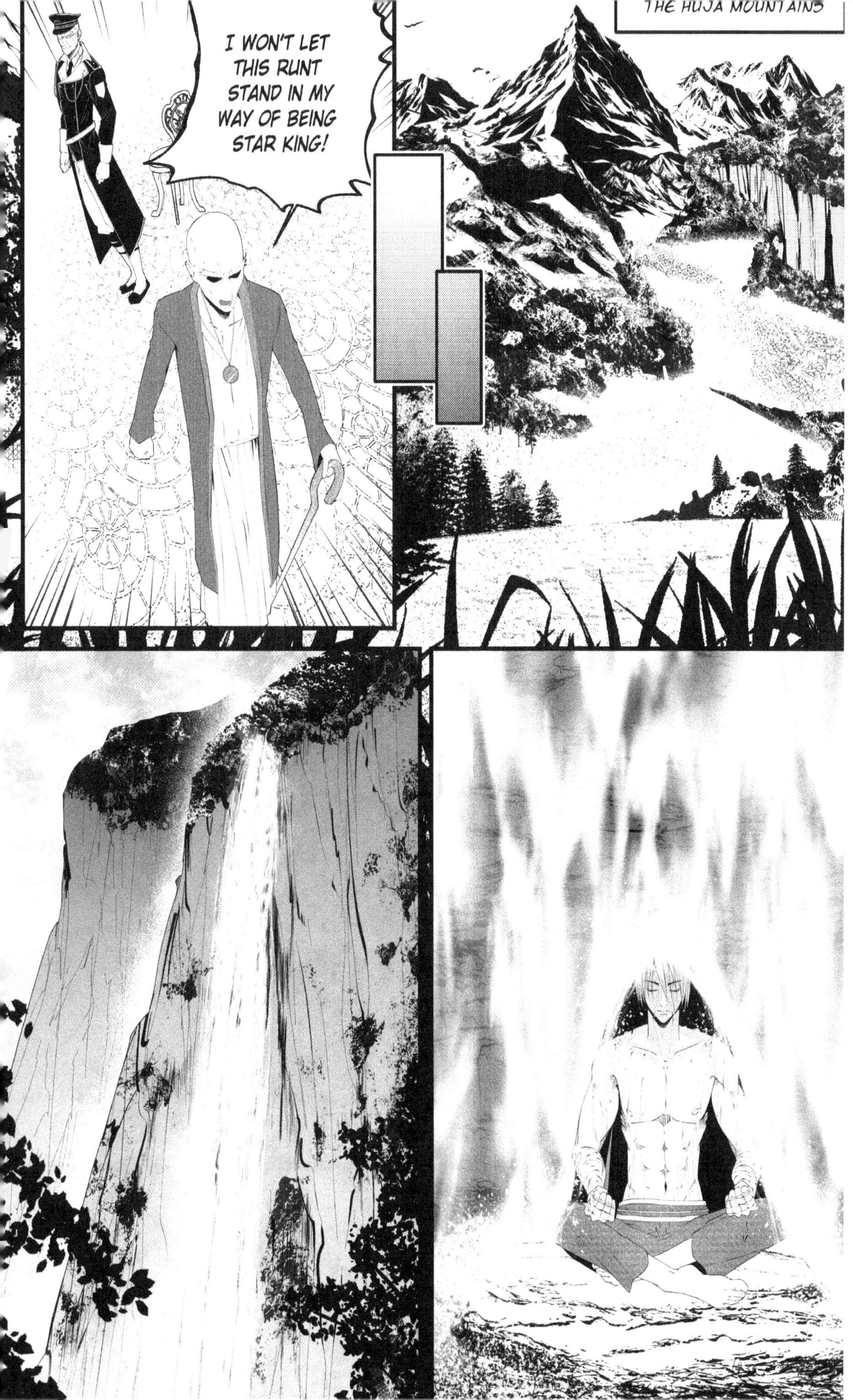

THE HUJA MOUNTAINS
I WON'T LET THIS RUNT STAND IN MY WAY OF BEING STAR KING!

SIR..
SOME B

I HOPE THIS DOESN'T TAKE LONG.

DON'T WORRY. IT WONT.

SO WHAT CAN I DO THE UNEXPECTED VISIT? SOMETHING TROUBLING YOU?
YOU CAN S THAT, I NE TO MAKE IMPACT WITH SELECTION STAR KIN BACK O
AH YES, YOU DO HAVE YOUR SIGHTS ON THAT. WELL YOU'RE GONNA HAVE TO REALLY SHOCK THE WORLD.
RUSTLE
RUSTLE
RIGHT NOW, NIGHTSTAR IS TOP TALK NOW.
I GOT YOU NOW !!!

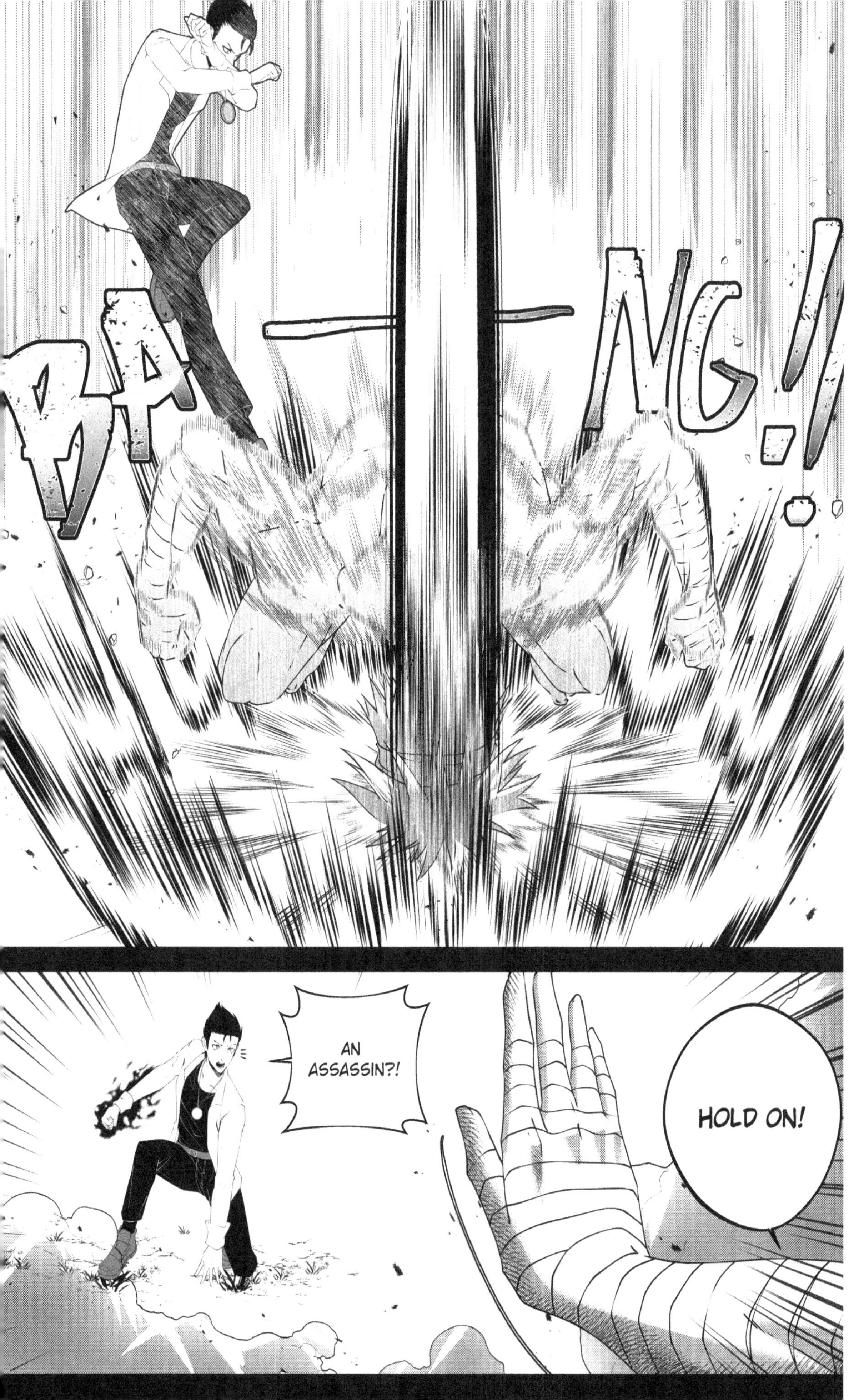

BA
NG!!
AN ASSASSIN?!
HOLD ON!

THIS IS JUST MY KNIGHT.
AS FOR YOUR PROBLEM.
IT'S SIMPLE.
DON'T IGNORE ME!

YOU JUST HAVE TO SHAKE THE WORLD EVEN HARDER THAN HIM.
TO BE CONTINUED

JEARED!!
JUST ACCEPT KEITH'S LOVE!

BEAL, YOU CAN'T READ AND THAT COMIC IS ABOUT A GIRL PRETENDING TO BE A GUY.

ARE YOU KIDDING ME?!
THERE GOES OUR FOOD..
I TOLD YOU THE EEL BURNS QUICK.
POP
POP
FORGET IT, YOU COOK FOR NOW ON!
SLAM
MERA, HOW MANY ATTEMPTS DID YOU HAVE?
EHHH.
YOU COULD OF SAID SOMETHING BEFORE YOU BURNT ALL OUR FOOD!

WILL YOU GUYS KEEP IT DOWN BACK THERE?!
BUT SHE BURNT ALL OF OUR FOOD. WE'RE GONNA STARVE.
HMM.
WE NEED TO STOP AND PICK UP FOOD SY.
UGH GUYS...
. . . .

WE DON'T HAVE THAT MUCH GEM LEFT..
YOU KNOW WE COULD MAKE THAT GEM LAST LONGER.
WE'RE NOT THIEVES.
JUST SAYING.
GUESS WE'LL HAVE TO MAKE DUE.
WE'LL JUST HAVE A QUICK STOP AND GO OK.

PORT VALES
CHATTER
CHATTER
CHATTER
CHATTER

WOW!
THAT'S THE
OCEAN!?
THIS BREEZE
FEELS AMAZING.
HOLD IT,
WE STILL
GOT TO BUY
SUPPLIES.
AW COME ON,
YOU GUYS
CAN DO THAT.
GRAB
PORT VALES,
LETS GO CHECK OUT
THE OCEAN!

HE'S RIGHT. WE NEED TO BE CAREFUL WITH OUR SPENDING.
SNATCH
I THINK I CAN GET THE MOST OUT OF MY STACK.
YOU THEIF! GIVE ME BACK THAT GEM!
WOOSH
WOOSH
HE HAS A POINT, SPREADING OUT TO GET FOOD WILL CUT OUR TIME HERE.
GRR!
DON'T TAKE HIS SIDE!

SHE JUST NEEDS TO COOL DOWN.
WELL LET'S GO SEE THAT OCEAN!
-GRAB-
NOT SO FAST.
SWIPE
YOU HAVE TO STAY HIDDEN.
FINE..
YOU KNOW IT'S HARD TO BE A CROWN IF I'M ALWAYS HIDING.
GOOD POINT.
YOU'RE ALSO A WANTED MAN.

CAPITAL BUILDING
NOW WHAT IS IT THAT YOU'RE CALLING ME FOR?
THIS ISN'T A JOKE SWAGGER.
I ALREADY ALERTED COMMAND, NIGHTSTAR IS IN YOUR AREA!
YO
WOR
TOO M
PEA

YOU SEE..
ALL WILL SUBMIT TO LAW.
ORDER OF LAW CAPTAIN: LAW SWAGGER

WHAT'S GOING ON HERE?
CHATTER
CHATTER
CHATTER
WHY DO THEY TAKE HIS SIDE?
GIVE ME ANOTH !!
MAN, SHE CAN REALLY PUT IT AWAY.

ANOTHER AND KEEP IT COMING.
GLUG
GLUG
GLUG
PAH
DUMBASS.
HUH..YOU THINK YOU CAN TAKE ME ON?
DROP

I LIKE THE CUT OF YOUR GIBS.

SOMEONE FIX US A COUPLE OF PLATES!

READY..

DON'T DISAPPOINT ME.

I WAS GONNA SAY THE SAME THING.

MARKET VENUE
WOW! IT'S THE OCEAN!
IT IS NICE TO SEE.
WE'LL HE... TO A BEA... AFTER... WE GE... SOME ... THE FO... MERA... BURNT...
I SHOULD OF SEEN THAT COMING..
SECURITY
ORDER OF LAW HUNTER: LUKE
CHATTER
CHATTER
CHATTER

I NEVER WANTED TO TAKE THIS POST.

WANTED
LOST

NOTHING EXCITING EVER HAPPENS IN THE MARKET..

THIS PLACE IS SO CROWDED.

WANTED
REWARD
50,000,000
GEM BOUNTY

WHAT IS H
DOING HERE
HE'S GONN
LEVEL THE
TOWN IF I
DON'T CAL
COMMAND

I DON'T NEED ANYTHING THAT EXCITING!

WOW..
IT'S BEAUTIFUL.
THE WATER IS SO BLUE.
I'M SO GETTING IN THE WATER.
HUH?
-CLICK-

..UM..COME..
W-WITH ME..
PLEASE?

?

...OK.

SLAM

ALRIGHT I CAUGHT NIGHTSTAR!! WAIT TILL CAPTAIN SWAGGER HEARS ABOUT THIS!

I COULD BE PROMOTED TO CAPTAIN FOR SURE.

MAYBE EVEN A SEAT AT THE HIGH COUNCEL!

WAIT TILL I TELL THE CAPTAIN!

THEY'RE GONNA BE MAD IF I STAY HERE.
SO THEY CAUGHT YOU TOO.. EH?
YEAH, THE GUY WHO CAUGHT ME LOOKED SO SCARED I JUST FOLLOWED HIM.
WAIT, SO YOU LET HIM CATCH YOU?
YEAH I SORT OF DID.

HOW CAN YOU BE SO CALM SWAGGER?!
BECAUSE EAIRLIER I WAS ABLE TO CAPTURE ONE OF THE TOP 10 MOST WANTED.
WHAT'S ONE MORE TO THE LIST.
.....
HAHAHA
HAHAHA
HAHAHA

YOU REALLY ARE A STRANGE ONE!
OSCAR REI
BOUNTY: 800,000,000
TO BE CONTINU

WHAT ARE YOU DOING?
WRITING.

I JUST WANTED TO WRITE MY THOUGHTS DOWN.
...NEEDS PICTURES.

HOW LONG BEFORE YOU GET THE CAMERA FIX BENNY?
......
I MEAN WE NEED THAT CAMERA TO BE READY IN CASE WE HEAR ANY NEWS.
....
BENNY LOOK!
....
NIGHT STAR
CHAPTER 18
I SWEAR I'VE SEEN THO MARKINGS BEF

WAIT I KNOW WHO THEY ARE..
THAT'S PIRATE KING OSCAR'S CREW!

PAK
YOU CAN PUT IT AWAY.
SO CAN YOU.
THE POT IS ALREADY AT 1,000 GEM.
HEY GIRL.

GET DOWN!!
SLASH

YOU'RE ONE CRAZY BASTARD. YOU KNOW THAT RIGHT?
WELL GET USE TO BEING HERE BEFORE THEY SEND US TO LIMBO.
HA HA
HA HA
WELL I'M GETTING BACK TO MY FRIENDS BEFORE THEY WORRY.
HOW DID YOU GET OUT?!
A FRIEND OF MINE SHOWED ME HOW TO PICK LOCKS.
WAIT HOLD ON.
MIND H A PAL

....
I GUESS I BETTER GET TO RAGO, HE SHOULD OF ENJOYED THE OCEAN ENOUGH.
..HUH?
GET BACK HERE!!
EEK!!
DERRICK?!
WHAT DID YOU DO?!

YOU WON'T GET AWAY.
PUFFFF
FIRST MATE OF THE STORM PIRATES: SILVIS
GRAB
FWOO
THAT WAS CLOSE.

WHAT DID YOU DO?!
GULP
YOUR FRIEND THERE STOLE FROM US. NO ONE STEALS FROM THE WIND PIRATES.
PFF, I DID.
SHUT IT, ALRIGHT.
FORGIVE MY FRIEND. HE'S AN IDIOT.
I TRIED PLEADING, THAT DIDN' WORK.

OH WHAT THE HECK NOW?
BOOM!
SOUNDS LIKE SAM HAS FINISHED HER DRINKS.
WE GOT TO GET OUT OF THE TOWN.
YEAH, I HAVE A BAD FEELING.
WE BETTER GET OUT OF HERE BEFORE THE DRONES ARRIVE.

WELL GOOD NEWS THEN BAD NEWS!
OUT WITH IT BOY!
WELL, I FOUND NIGHTSTAR IN THE CITY, THEN I CAPTURED HIM AND LOCKED HIM UP WITH THE OTHER PRISONER AND NOW..
THEY ESCAPED..
WHAT?!

ACTIVATE THE DRONES, THEY WONT GET FAR.
NOTIFY UN TO CON TO LOCA
I'M IN PURSUIT.

THAT'S WHAT I CALL AN EXIT.
DON'T YOU THINK YOU WENT A BIT FAR?
CRASH
WHAT NOW?
THESE GUYS AGAIN.

CRAP.
ONE IS H
THAN LA
TCH
MERA?!
WHAT ARE
YOU DOING?
LET'S
PUSH
GUY

THESE GUYS
ARE TOUGH.

IF THAT'S THE CASE THEN WE'LL JUST HIT 'EM HARD.
THANKS, I OWE YOU ONE.
I JUST GOT TO FIND MY CREW.
I NEED TO FIND MY FRIENDS.
WHAT'S WITH THE HOOD ON YOUR HEAD?
OH, T TO K A L PRO
WAIT, WAIT, WAIT

ARE YOU SERIOUS, YOU'RE A CROWN?!
YOU SHOULD BE PLASTERING YOUR FLAG!
DON'T YOU WANT TO BE STAR KING?!
UGH, I DO.
THEN LET THE WORLD KNOW YOUR PRESENCE!
YES I'M GONNA BE STAR KING!
COME ON LET ME HEAR IT!
THAT WAS EASY

SO WE MEET AT LAST, NIGHTSTAR.
TO BE CONTINUED.

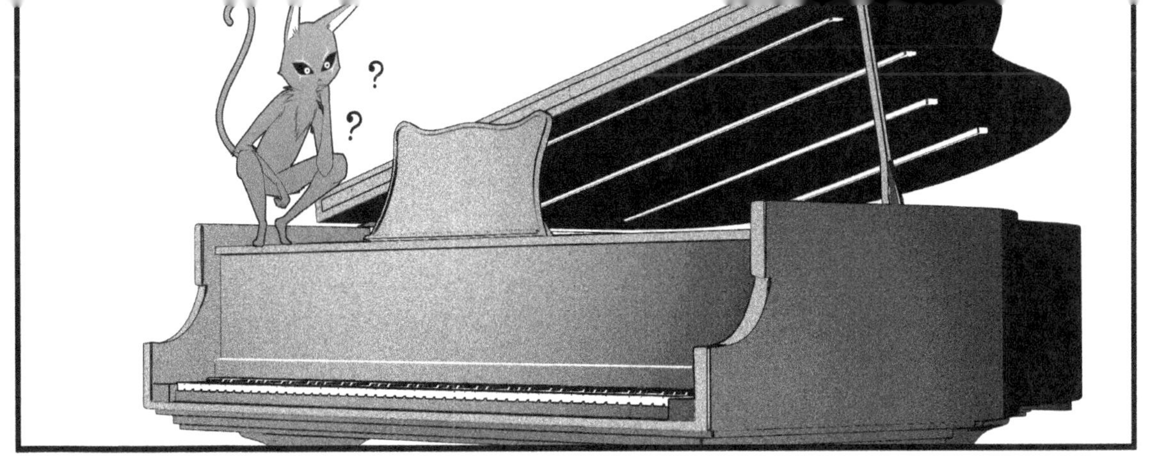

?
?
?

!!

FOR THOSE WHO CAN'T HEAR MUSIC, HE'S PLAYING IT REALLY BAD.

NIGHT STAR
CHAPTER 19
I DIDN'T EXPECT THE CAPTAIN TO FIND US SO QUICK.
JUST WHO IS THIS GUY?
I DONT WANT TO FIGHT YOU BUT I WILL IF I HAVE TO.
I FORGOT TO MENTION HE CAN STEAL ABILITIES.
CAPTAIN LAW SWAGGER, HE'S DANGERIOUS
YOU COULD OF TOLD ME THAT SOONER!
AW FLATTERY WILL GET YOU NOWHERE.

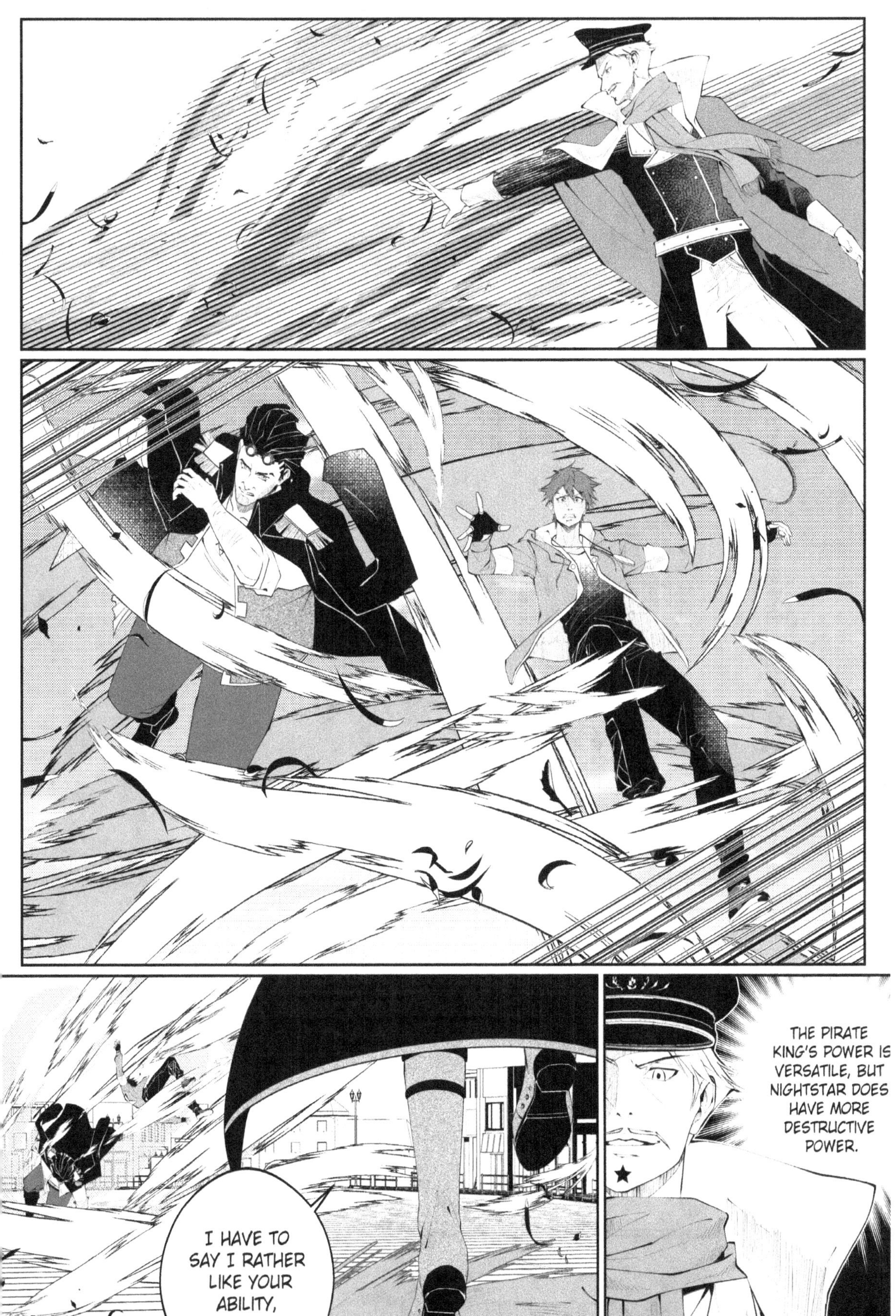
THE PIRATE KING'S POWER IS VERSATILE, BUT NIGHTSTAR DOES HAVE MORE DESTRUCTIVE POWER.
I HAVE TO SAY I RATHER LIKE YOUR ABILITY, PIRATE KING.

I'LL HAVE TO TRY IT OUT!
LOOK OUT!
SWIPE
I GOT IT!

MAYBE THAT WAS TOO MUCH.
I MAY NEED SOME HELP WITH THIS ONE.
→CLICK←
WHAT NOW?!

WHAT IS THAT?!
IT'S ONE OF THE ORDER OF LAW'S HUNTING DROID.
I KNOW I'M SUPPOSED TO BE SCARED BUT THAT'S COOL!
I KNOW RIGHT!
CAPTURE THEM!
GLARE

UGH.. RAGO?

CRAP, HOLD ON!
ON YOUR GUARD PIRATE!

SPIN
OOF!

DON'T MOVE YOU'LL BE BACK IN A CELL SOON ENOUGH.
NOW LETS SEE JUST HOW DESTRUCTIVE YOUR ABILITES ARE.
I WONDER WHAT I CAN DO WITH YOUR ABILITY.. NIGHTSTAR.

WHAT IS THIS....
POWER?!
HIS ABILITY
IT REJECTE
ME?

OH NO?!
I LET GO!

LOOKS LIKE
YOU CAN ONLY
HOLD ONE
ABILITY
AT A TIME.

I.. DON
WHY I
STEAL
ABILIT
WON'T
GET

THERE THEY ARE!
HUH?
IT'S THE CAPTAIN!
RAGO OVER HERE!
CHATTER
CHATTER
CHATTER
CAUSING MORE TROUBLE I SEE.
THIS TIME I DIDN'T START IT I SWEAR.
THERE'S MORE OF THEM.
DX-2 APPREHEND THOSE--!!
CRASH
I KNOW THAT WINDSTREAM ANYWHERE.

GUYS! WHAT ARE YOU DOING HERE?

SEE I KNOW MY CAPTAIN.

CAPTAIN SWAGGER NEEDS OUR SUPPORT, COME ON!

I WILL NOT HAVE MY NAME TARNISHED BY YOU LOWLY SWINE.

HEY RAGO, HOW ABOUT I PAY YOU BACK.

WHAT DO YOU MEAN?
WE'LL HANDLE THINGS HERE. TIME FOR SOME PAYBACK BOYS!
AYE!
COME ON, IT WOULD BE BEST IF WE DO AS HE SAYS.
RIGHT
NOD

SURE IT'S OK TO LET THEM GO?
I'M GONNA MISS MY EATING BUDDY.
HEY CAPTAIN!!
ARE YOU INSANE?!
HOW'S THIS FOR SHOWING THE WORLD!
HA HA HAHA
HAHA H
NOW THAT'S A KING!
YOU READY CAPTAIN?
OH YEAH

SO WHAT WAS THAT DISPLAY AT THE PORT?
I THINK I HAD ENOUGH OF THE OCEAN FOR ONE DAY

CAPTAIN SAID THAT I NEEDED TO SHOW THE WORLD THAT I WANNA BECOME STAR KING.

DOING THAT REQUIRES US TO HAVE TERRITORIES, ALLIANCES, WAYS TO SHOW THAT WE CAN BE A FORCE.

MAN B
STAR
IS A
OF W

WHOA! BENNY PLEASE TELL ME YOU GOT SOME OF THAT ON FILM.
-NODS-
HOLD IT BENNY.

DAMN..
I CAN'T BELIEVE I LOST BOTH OF THEM.
MEN, I WANT A REPORT ON THE DAMAGE AND SOMEONE TO ALERT COMMAND.
THEY GOT AWAY.
TO BE CONTINUE

MONROE, IS IT TUESDAY ALREADY?!
YUP.
STILL WEIGHTS THE SAME?
AS MUCH AS YOU CAN BARE.

I APPRECIATE YOU DOING THIS FOR ME ROE.
NO PROBLEM.

VITRO CASTLE
I CAN'T BELIEVE THAT WOMAN.
ACTING SO HIGH AND MIGHTY TO ME. NO MATTER, I HAVE MORE IMPORTANT THINGS TO ATTEND TO.
HAHAHA HAHAHA
WHAT ARE YOU KACKLING AT?

JUST TO SEE THE LOOK ON YOUR FACE WHEN YOU READ THIS.

WHAT?!! NIGHTSTAR HAS TAKEN OUT THE MAYOR OF ROMA TOWN AND RUNNING A MUCK IN MY TERRITORIES?!

SIR, DON'T WASTE YOUR BREATH WITH THIS BEAST.

OBVIOUSLY HE DOESN'T TAKE HIS JOB SERIOUSLY. IF YOU WANT, I WILL GRAB THIS NIGHTSTAR.

KNIGHT OF THE CROWN CHARLES: KANE SALONE

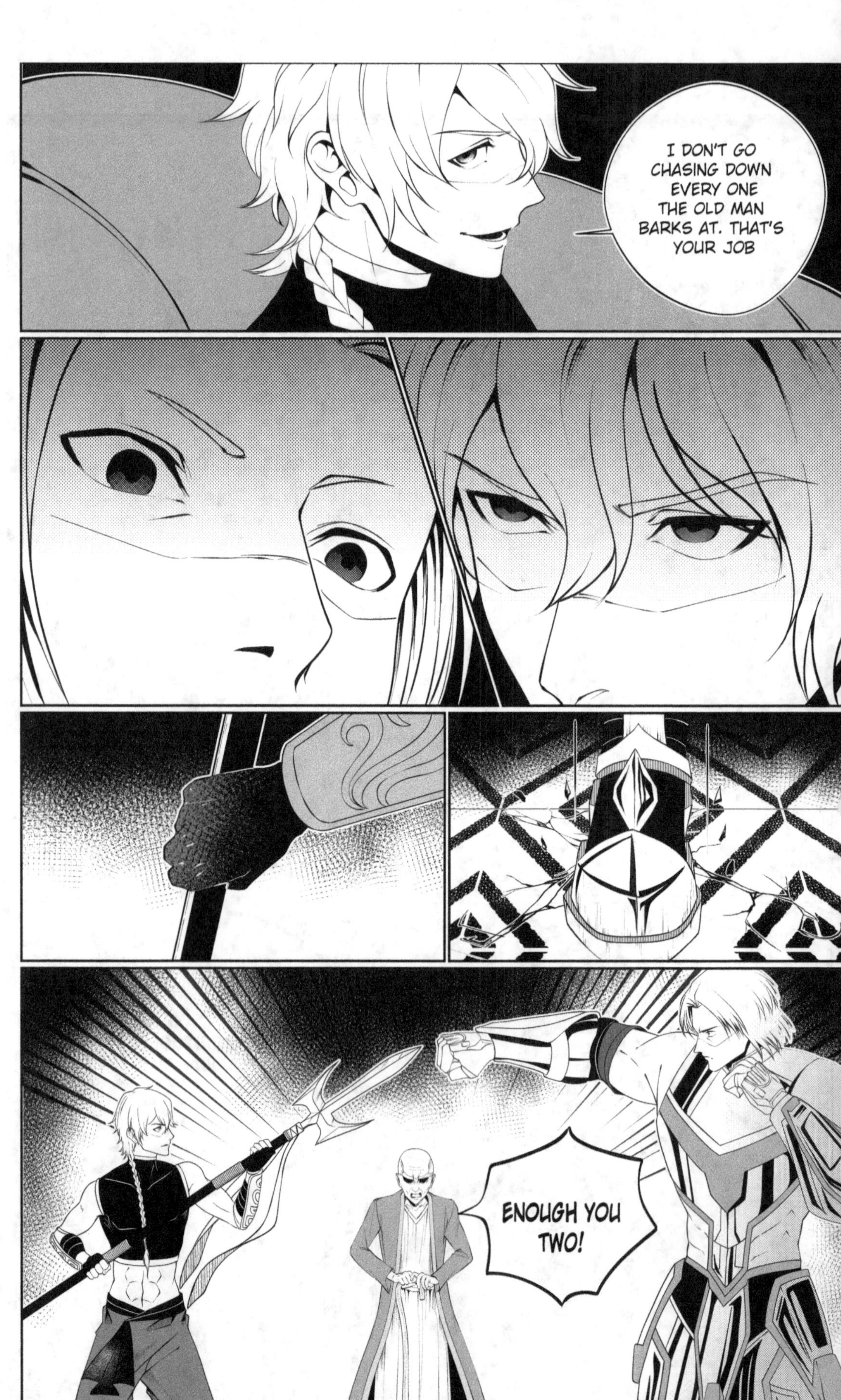

I DON'T GO CHASING DOWN EVERY ONE THE OLD MAN BARKS AT. THAT'S YOUR JOB
ENOUGH YOU TWO!

I DON'T NEED YOU TWO TEARING UP THE CASTLE WITH YOUR PETTY SQUABBLE.
BUT SIR--
IF I SEND YOU THEN I WILL BE ACKNOWLEDGING THAT NIGHTSTAR IS A THREAT TO ME.

I WILL SPEAK WITH THE ORDER OF LAW ABOUT THIS.

YOU SHOULD TAKE YOUR TITLE OF BEAST SERIOUSLY.
TELL YOU WHAT, IF NIGHTSTAR TAKES YOU DOWN.

THEN I'LL TAKE HIM DOWN MYSELF.
ONE OF THE 7 BEAST: THE DRAGON: JAKE FU

SY DO YOU THINK YOU CAN MAKE US ONE OF THOSE DRONES?
WE WOULD BE A FORCE TO BE RECKONED WITH IF WE HAD THAT.
I DON'T HAVE THE EQUIPMENT OR THE KNOW HOW TO MAKE ONE OF THOSE THINGS.
WE WOULDN'T BE ABLE KEEP IT ANYWHERE TILL WE GET TO NOVA.
SO HOW LONG DO YOU THINK IT WILL TAKE US TO GET TO NOVA CAPITAL?
NOT SURE, WE HAVE TIME UNTIL THE SUMMIT, BUT AT OUR RATE TWO MONTHS.
WISH THAT SHADOW LADY COULD TELL US.

YOU RINGED FOR ME MY CROWN?
WHO IS SHE?
I'M RAG SHADO
WAIT YOU'VE BEEN HERE THIS ENTIRE TIME?
THEN, WHICH DIRECTION IS BEST TO REACH NOVA?
AS YOUR SHADOW, I'M ALWAYS HERE TO ASSIST YOU.

HEADING TOWARDS THE LU-KA-LU FOREST IS FASTEST.
WHA--
SO ARE YOU TRAVELING WITH US NOW?
I PREFER TO WATCH YOU FROM A DISTANCE. UNLESS YOU WANT ME TO STAY AROUND.

YOU CAN DO WHAT YOU FEEL IS BEST.
I DON'T WANT TO FORCE YOU TO DO SOMETHING UNCOMFORTABLE

THANK YOU.
FWOOOOSH
WAIT RAGO, THAT FOREST IS DEEP AND FULL OF TREES, THE ROVER WONT FIT. WE MIGHT JUST GO AROUND.
ALRIGHT TO THE LU-KA-LU FOREST THEN!
THAT WILL TAKE A DAY LONGER.
EITHER WAY IT'S YOUR CALL RAGO.
WE GOT ENOUGH SUPPLIES FOR BOTH OPTIONS

. . . .
LET'S JUST HEAD STRAIGHT THROUGH, ANY TREES IN OUR WAY WE'LL JUST KNOCK EM DOWN!
FINE.
HERE WE ARE.

WHOA
THIS PLACE
IS HUGE!
THE LU-KA-LU FOREST

WHOA, MY NECK IS GETTING TIRED.
YEAH, WHO KNEW TREES GET THIS TALL.
I WANT TO CLIMB THE TOP SO BAD!
STILL THINK WE CAN KNOCK DOWN A TREE?

FOREST PIRATES!
RUSTLE
RUSTLE
I DON'T LIKE THE LOOK OF THIS.
JA-ME-HU MA.

WHAT DID HE SAY?
NOT SURE BUT I FEEL LIKE I HEARD SOMETHING THAT BEFORE.
KA-LU SUME NALA JA KIN.
YAAAAAAAAA
YAAAAAAAAAA-AAAAAAAAAAAA!!

JA
KIN
!!!
RATTLE
RATTLE
RATTLE
RATTLE
MERA? WHAT WAS-
I'LL DIRECT SYRUS TO FOLLOW HIM.
MERA IF SOMETHING IS WRONG, TELL ME.
THIS IS MY HOME. WELCOME TO THE BARI TRIBE.

STILL.
DON'T WORRY SHE PROBABLY HAD A FALL OUT WITH HER FAMILY.
WAIT WHY AREN'T YOU JUMPING FOR JOY? WE'RE GOING TO A VILLAGE, WITH VILLAGE WOMEN.
YEAH BUT IT'S MERA'S VILLAGE.
WHAT IF MERA IS THE CREAM OF THE CROP AND EVERYONE ELSE IS JUST SECOND CLASS.
YEAH I DON'T THINK SO.
WE'RE HERE.
WOW THIS PLACE IS AMAZING!
HOW AMAZING ARE TREES AND ROCKS?
GULP

WELCOME TO MY HOME.

I MAY NEVER LEAVE.
I HAVE TO ADMIT THIS IS IMPRESSIVE.
YEAH IT'S LIKE SUMMER CAMP.
WELCOME FRIENDS, WE ARE PREPARING TO CELEBRATE TONIGHT.
WE MUST OF ARRIVED ON TIME FOR SOMETHING SPECIAL.
WHAT ARE WE CELEBRATING?
BUM
BUM
BUM

....

OUR KING IS IN GOOD SPIRITS TODAY.

KING OF THE BARI TRIBE: RESH

MERA YOU'VE RETURN TO US.
HI DAD.
I'M GLAD YOU'RE DOING ALRIGHT MY LITTLE KAKAFU
BARI ADVISOR: SALIM
YOU'RE MERA'S FATHER, AWESOME. I'M RAGO.
....
OH YOU'RE THE ONE WHO BROUGHT MERA BACK TO US. YOU HAVE MY THANKS.

I'M GLAD YOU HAVE RETURN MERA, NOW WE CAN CONTINUE WITH OUR PLANS AFTER OUR PARTY.
WHAT ARE YOU ALL CELEBRATING ANYWAY?

THE RETURN OF OUR QUEEN, MERA!!
WHAAAA!
TO BE CONTINUED.

Dear Reader,

From the bottom of my heart, thank you for your incredible support. Every page, every panel, and every story I create is possible because of you. Your love for this series fuels my passion and keeps me pushing forward, striving to bring you even more.

This journey isn't just mine—it's ours. We walk this road together, step by step, through every adventure, twist, and turn. Your belief in this series means the world to me, and I can't wait to share what's next.

Stay with me, and let's make something unforgettable.

Author's note 1

"I've received a lot of questions about Rago's appearance, and I'm not sure why. Since his very first conception, he has always had light brown skin and red hair—that's just been his defining look for the longest time. If Rago existed in the real world, I imagine he'd be in America. I never assigned him a specific race, and I think that's for the best."

Author's note 2

"When I first created the Order of Law, they were originally meant to be just another faction under a Crown. However, as I developed the world further, I realized there needed to be a dedicated police force—one that governs the world and upholds the law."